Monte

By

Dave and Pat Sargent

Illustrated by
Jane Lenoir

Ozark Publishing, Inc.
P.O. Box 228
Prairie Grove, AR 72753

Sargent, Dave, 1941-
   Monte / by Dave and Pat Sargent ; illustrated by Jane
Lenoir. — Prairie Grove, AR : Ozark Publishing, ©2001.
   ix, 36 p. : col. ill. ; 23 cm. (Saddle-up series)

   "Take pride in your work"—Cover.

   SUMMARY: Monte, the silver buckskin horse, works
hard on a Colorado ranch herding cattle, but one memorable
day he has to corral a mother pig and her six squealing
babies. Includes factual information on buckskin horses.
   ISBN: 1-56763-657-8   (hc)
            1-56763-658-6 (pbk)

   [1. Horses—Fiction. 2. Ranch life—Fiction.] I. Sargent,
Pat, 1936- II. Lenoir, Jane, 1950- ill. III. Title.
IV. Series.

   PZ10.3. S243Mon 2001
   [E]—dc21   2001-002984

Printed in the United States of America

iv

Inspired by

an occasional sighting of a silver buckskin. Most buckskins we see have yellow coats with black points, but the silver buckskin is a pretty creamy color with no other marks.

Dedicated to

our very special friends who raise buckskin horses.

Foreword

When blasts of winter winds on the beautiful Colorado plains send the temperature down to below freezing, Boss Slim Walker takes his horse, Monte, to round up some silly cow critters and their calves. One little calf is stubborn and does not want to be put into the corral. Before Boss Slim can shut the gate, the ornery calf whirls and takes off. Monte is determined to get the calf into the corral with the others so that he can eat his ration of oats and hay.

The fun begins when Slim ropes a mama pig with six howling babies. Slim wants to get them home, but Monte balks! He's a cow horse! Is he really expected to deal with a squealing pig and her babies?

Contents

Monte

If you would like to have the authors of the Saddle Up Series visit your school, free of charge, call 1-800-321-5671 or 1-800-960-3876.

One

The Blinding Snow

A sudden blast of cold wind over the plains of Colorado sent the temperature to below freezing. The late afternoon sky was soon filled with a big bank of clouds, and a light snow began to fall.

"Brrrr," the silver buckskin said with a smile as Slim Walker entered the corral. "I'm sure glad to see you, Boss. That barn and those oats will make my life a whole lot better."

The determined expression on Slim's face told Monte that a warm barn and oats were not in the man's plans.

"Oh no," the silver buckskin groaned. "Boss probably wants us to gather up those silly cow critters and put them in the corral. I don't know why they won't come in by themselves."

Minutes later, Monte carried his boss across the prairie in a fast lope. Through the blinding snow, the horse and rider slowly gathered the herd into one large bunch and started back toward the barn and corrals. As the cows and calves were trotting through the open gate, one little calf glanced up at Monte and grinned. Then he whirled around and took off running away from the corral.

"You young whippersnapper," the silver buckskin yelled as he spun

around. "Come back here! It's too
cold and miserable to play games."

As Monte raced after the calf, he heard Slim chuckling.

"Monte," he said. "You're the only horse I know that can turn on a dime and give a fellow a nickel in change."

The silver buckskin was too busy and upset with the ornery calf to hear Slim. His ears were flat against his head, and his gaze never left the running calf. Then to make matters worse, the critter suddenly stopped and whirled around.

"That was a real sneaky move," Monte muttered, "but not sneaky enough."

The silver buckskin again spun around to face the calf. The little critter dodged and ducked back and forth, but Monte was in front of him with every turn.

"Are you ready to give up?"
Monte asked through clenched teeth.
"Or do you want to play this game?"
 The calf shook his head and
trotted back toward the corral.

"Well, Monte," Slim said as he closed the gate to the big corral. "You did a good job of getting every one of those cows and calves in. Now it's your turn for a warm barn and a big helping of oats."

"Thanks, Boss," Monte replied. "I'm sure ready for that."

Minutes later, he was unsaddled and quietly munching on fresh hay and a big helping of oats.

"Sorry I couldn't help you," the dappled grey in the adjoining stall said, "but my boss is not here. He took the black sabino to the general store in town to get some supplies."

"Thanks for the thought but we made short work of getting those crazy cow critters in today," Monte said between bites. "I really like gathering and sorting cattle," he said with a grin, "but not in a blizzard."

"I know what you mean," the dappled grey agreed with a chuckle. "It's kind of fun when the weather is nice and warm."

The next two months of winter passed rather quickly for Monte the Silver Buckskin. Every day was filled with work that he loved. From gathering and sorting to roping and moving cow critters, he knew in his heart that his life was full and good.

"Don't tell Boss," he said to the dappled grey one evening, "but I like ranch life even during cold winter months."

"I won't," the dappled grey said with a grin. "He'll think you're loco and cut down your ration of oats."

"That's right," Monte agreed with a nod, "and I don't want that!"

Within minutes, the two horses were dozing peacefully. They both needed to be rested and alert in the morning to begin another day of work on the ranch.

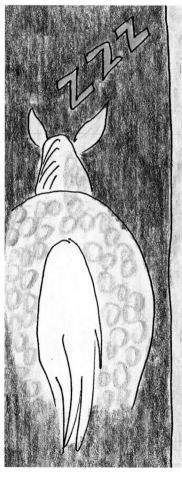

Two

The Runaway

Monte smiled as he looked at the new leaves on the trees. Hmmm, he thought. Springtime is without a doubt my favorite part of the year. The grass is getting green and lush again. He watched Slim leave the house and walk toward the corral.

"Morning, Boss," he nickered. "This is one fine day, isn't it? What are we going to do with it? It's too nice a day to stand around."

Slim entered the corral with a big grin on his face.

"Well, Monte," he said, "can you feel it, boy? It looks like spring is finally here. It feels good, doesn't it? I think you and I will make a run up to the north country today and check for stray cattle. How does that sound to you?"

Monte whinnied and nodded his head up and down. Actually, he was getting very excited. He loved the view from the hills. He stomped his front hoof. He was raring to go!

Within a short time, the horse and rider were traveling past the clumps of sagebrush and soapweed in a slow, easy trot. I sure do love this country, Monte thought as he reached the top of a hill. He glanced down at the lake below, and his heart beat a little faster as he scanned the horizon of the Colorado plains.

"I can see a thousand miles," he said. "I know that's not possible, but I can see the big buffalo wallow in the north pasture from here."

Suddenly he saw something
dart through the small trees growing
beside the lake.

"Uh oh," Slim said in a slow drawl. "I think we've just found the runaway, Monte."

"Runaway?" Monte repeated. "I didn't know we had any runaways. Why would any critter want to leave your ranch, Boss? There's plenty of feed and a safe place to sleep."

Slim nudged Monte with the heels of his boots and muttered, "We better go check this out."

As they descended the hill, they heard a strange sound.

"That doesn't sound like a cow critter to me, Boss," Monte said. "I don't know what it is."

Slim reined him to a halt. He was staring at a tamarack tree in the distance when a varmint suddenly darted into view.

"There she is, Monte!" Slim yelled. "Let's go get her!"

The big silver buckskin lunged forward as he muttered, "Why, I don't see a cow critter in sight, Boss. Have you lost your mind?"

"Oink! Oink! Oink!" the varmint squealed as she darted out of sight again.

Suddenly Monte saw six little critters scamper amid the tamaracks.

"Good grief, Boss," he groaned. "I'm a cutting horse, a fast horse, a sorting horse, a super good ranch horse and partner. But," he groaned, "I don't know how to handle a pig and her half-grown younguns!"

Slim uncoiled his rope and made a big loop. He nudged Monte with the heels of his boots and yelled, "Let's go get her!"

"Oh, dear," the silver buckskin groaned as he leaped into action. "I don't like this."

The mama pig hit a dead run in seconds. She darted through the tamaracks with the six babies squealing and racing behind her. Slim nudged Monte again with the heel of his boots.

"Come on, Monte," Slim said, "just pretend she's a calf."

"Yeah, right!" Monte groaned. "I just don't have that kind of an imagination. She's a loud squealer, and I don't want her tied to me."

For several minutes, the mama pig, her six bawling kids, and Monte dodged in and around the short, scrubby trees.

Finally the mama pig turned toward the open prairie. Her shrieks of anger echoed against the quiet spring day. Slim swung the loop of the rope over his head until Monte put him within throwing distance.

The rope sailed through the air and gracefully landed over the head of the pig. As Slim pulled up the slack in the rope, she accidentally stuck one leg through the loop.

Three

The Howling Pigs

Monte skidded to a halt, and the rope between the mama pig and him jerked tight.

"Oink! Oink! Oink! Oink!" she screamed.

For just a split second, Monte considered throwing a tantrum.

As he tensed his body, Slim quietly said, "Easy, boy. Easy now. It's going to be okay. She's just a bit loud, that's all."

"A bit loud?" Monte yelled. "Good grief, Boss!" He glared at the captured pig and growled, "Will you please stop that awful noise? You're hurting my ears!"

The silver buckskin stared at the mama pig. His ears were pointed straight at her as he stepped forward and back to keep the rope tight between them.

A minute later, the mama pig stopped yelling and stared at Monte. Her six babies glanced at her, and then they, too, stopped yelling.

"Whew," Monte murmured. "Silence is wonderful."

Slim chuckled and said, "Well, this is nice, but we'll never get her home unless we start moving in that direction."

"Oh no, Boss," Monte groaned. "Do we have to? I really don't mind hanging around here for a while."

"It won't take us long to get home," Slim said, "once we start heading that way."

Where is that dappled grey friend of mine? the silver buckskin thought. He never seems to be around when I need him.

His ears went flat against the back of his head as he growled, "Okay, Boss, but you sure do owe me on this one."

He slowly turned toward home. The mama pig skidded on her hooves behind him, squealing once again at the top of her lungs. The six younguns trotted beside her, howling and crying every step of the way.

"This is embarrassing, Boss," the silver buckskin mumbled as he slowly walked toward home with the mama pig skidding along behind him. A moment later, he murmured, "I guess it won't matter as long as nobody sees me."

Suddenly he saw the dappled grey and his boss loping toward him.

"Now it matters!" he said in a loud tone of voice. "Come on, Boss. Cut her loose."

As the dappled grey skidded to a halt in front of him, Slim laughed and said, "What do you think of this cow critter that Monte and I just caught, Joe? Will she make prime beef one of these days?"

Monte and the dappled grey stared at each other as their bosses laughed.

"So! Where have you been?" Monte asked. "You always seem to have business someplace else when I need you."

The dappled grey grinned. "We've been doctoring some sick calves in the south pasture," he said. "It was nothing compared to your outstanding ranch duties."

Monte glared at him as he moved forward with the howling pigs trailing behind.

"I have to hand it to you, Slim," Joe said with a chuckle. "I'm not sure if this dappled grey and I would have attempted bringing a runaway pig and her younguns back home."

"Well," Slim muttered. "It was a strange catch, Joe. The loop is over her head and one front foot." He grinned as he added, "And we could not get the rope off her."

"It takes a good cowboy," Joe said with a chuckle, "to rope a pig."

"Humph," Monte muttered. "It takes a crazy cowboy to rope one, and a loco horse to take one home."

An hour later, the mama pig and her six younguns were munching on good feed. The ranch was peaceful and quiet for the first time since early morning. Slim gave Monte an extra helping of oats and hay after unsaddling him, and Monte could hear Slim's happy whistle echoing within the barn as he left the stall.

Hmmm, Monte thought as he took a big bite of fresh oats. Good cow horses should have a place of their own in history. He smiled as he quietly corrected his thoughts.

"Ranch horse!" he exclaimed. "I am not a cow horse," he said. "I am a good ranch horse, and proud of it! Life on the ranch is good and getting more exciting every day!"

Four

Silver Buckskin Facts

There is confusion concerning the *buckskin* horse color.

Some horses in the buckskin group have primitive marks on them, others do not. Sometimes, horsemen call horses with yellow bodies, black points, and primitive marks *duns*. They call those without the marks *buckskins*. There are others who call horses without marks *duns*.

Today, groups of yellow-coated horses with black points are called buckskin.

The silver buckskins we have found have creamy body colors and no primitive marks.